Three One-Act Plays
About the Elderly

by Elyse Nass

A SAMUEL FRENCH ACTING EDITION

SAMUEL FRENCH
FOUNDED 1830

SAMUELFRENCH.COM

ISBN   978-0-573-69205-5   Printed in U.S.A.   #22698

MUSIC USE NOTE

IMPORTANT BILLING AND CREDIT REQUIREMENTS

SECOND CHANCE

Second Chance was presented by the Quaigh Theatre in New York City in 1978, under the direction of Kathleen Huber, with the following cast:

RITA...Elizabeth Abbassi
EVELYN ....Ruby Payne

A subsequent production was staged at the San Diego Repertory Theatre by their Senior Theatre Project, "Go Like 60," and then toured senior citizen centers in San Diego, California.

Additionally, the play has toured senior citizen centers in New York City, been produced in community theatres, and was televised on cable TV in Minnesota.

Second Chance was presented abroad in Singapore (in English) by TheatreWorks at The Drama Centre.

CHARACTERS

RITA   late sixties, vivacious,
                              trying to appear
                              buoyant.

EVELYN   mid-sixties, but she
                              looks tired and is
                              letting things take their
                              course.

TIME

The present. A spring evening.

PLACE

The nicely furnished living room of Rita's home, a
small apartment in New York City.

SECOND CHANCE

SCENE: The nicely furnished living room of Rita's home, a small apartment in New York City. There is a couch and two end tables: Table "A" and Table "B." On Table "A" is a telephone, address book, plastic jar of bubble liquid containing wand, a bottle of vitamins, and a copy of a playscript. On Table "B" are flowers in bowl (or vase). These flowers can be artificial. There is also a framed photograph of a man, "Charlie." NOTE: The positions of Table "A" and Table "B" can be reversed. Whatever its position, EVELYN should always be sitting beside table with phone, Table "A." If there are walls, they display old movie posters, family photographs, and theatrical memorabilia.

AT RISE: RITA is pacing around in a full-length caftan. Finally EVELYN knocks on door.

RITA. (*In British accent.*) Hurry up and enter!

(*EVELYN walks in. SHE is wearing a plain housedress.*)

RITA. I never thought you'd get here.

EVELYN. Why? I live right next door. What's the matter?

RITA. Please sit down.

EVELYN. Why?

RITA. You're all out of breath, so take a seat quickly. (*SHE pushes her down on couch.*)

EVELYN. I am not out of breath. What's going on?

RITA. Now just relax. (*SHE begins massaging Evelyn's temples.*)

EVELYN. Just what are you doing to my head?

RITA. Just massaging your temples to give you a sense of calmness.

EVELYN. I am calm. What's happening?

RITA. Breathe deeply—

EVELYN. Look, Rita. You better tell me what this is all about.

RITA. A calcium tablet is good for the nerves. Let me get—

EVELYN. No, I'm not taking anything. I want an explanation. Right now!

RITA. I only wanted to prepare you for the surprise.

EVELYN. Surprise?

RITA. Yes, the big surprise ... the revelation ... but you won't sit still for a minute ... So here we go ... But first close your eyes ...

(*EVELYN does so reluctantly. Now RITA takes off caftan and drapes it over the corner of the couch. SHE is wearing a flesh color leotard with matching tights ... or it can be a costume that's equally outrageous.)*

RITA. Now open them slowly—very slowly.

(EVELYN does so.)

RITA. Ta-ta!
EVELYN. *(Rises, doing a double-take.)* Oh, my God! What are you wearing?
RITA. It's my costume for the play.
EVELYN. That's your costume?
RITA. Yes, this is what I wear.
EVELYN. But it's so—so revealing.
RITA. It is not.
EVELYN. Oh, let me sit down. *(SHE does.)* I can't believe it. So that was the surprise?
RITA. I didn't realize you'd be so shocked.
EVELYN. Well, you told me about the play. I didn't expect you to look like that. You said you were a strange British grandmother who sits around blowing bubbles and eating Barricini chocolates.
RITA. Yes, and my whole family is all around me. My grandson believes he's a frog. My daughter goes back and forth to Mars.
EVELYN. And the people around you—how are they dressed?
RITA. In various ways. Some are clothed, some are—

EVELYN. I don't want to hear anymore. I'm living next door to a weirdo for twenty-five years and didn't know it till now.

RITA. Don't be such a prude. This is a different generation we're living in. It's the "now" generation.

EVELYN. Maybe for you, Rita. (*Pause.*) I don't think we'll be at the play. I mean George and I. He might have a heart attack seeing ... (*Pause.*) Is that what you made me rush in here for? To see you like this, like a—a woman of ill-repute.

RITA. I had no idea you'd be so shocked. I thought you were more up on the times. Evelyn, you better sit down for the second part.

EVELYN. Oh, no! Don't tell me you have to take that off?

RITA. No, it's nothing like that. (*Pause. SHE sits beside Evelyn.*) It's serious business, Evelyn. (*Pause.*) They're coming.

EVELYN. Who?

RITA. My children.

EVELYN. Your children?

RITA. Yes, they're coming to see me.

EVELYN. To see you?

RITA. Yes.

EVELYN. In the play?

RITA. No, not exactly. They're coming to spend the weekend with me. A year ago, Charlie died. So they don't want me to be alone. Now here I am opening in this play in the Village. My first part in a play—my acting debut!

EVELYN. And what a debut! You can't let them see you. Why, it's a sin that you're doing this. Now, I always thought you shouldn't be acting. But no, you insisted. So I thought, all right, you'll keep busy. Maybe it's for the best. But look what you're going to be in. You could be arrested wearing that ... and on this, of all weekends!

RITA. No, I won't be arrested. There's nothing wrong with how I look or with what I'm doing. It's a perfectly good avant-garde play.

EVELYN. But it's outrageous! To do it, on the first anniversary of your husband's death.

RITA. Let's not keep going over that, Evelyn. I've made up my mind to go through with this. And we've got to think of what to do.

EVELYN. What did you tell your children?

RITA. I told them they didn't have to come here. I said I would have company, I wouldn't be alone. But they insisted. What could I say?

EVELYN. Nothing. And you'll have to stay home with them, right here where you belong.

RITA. Evelyn!

EVELYN. That's right.

RITA. But I'm going to be busy—with run-throughs during the day. I won't have much time to spend with them.

EVELYN. This is a solemn time, Rita. How can you think of that play? The play doesn't matter. Lots of times, those things never go on.

RITA. Oh, but this will. The show must go on even if it's in a loft.

EVELYN. But what about Charlie's memory?

RITA. I've mourned him long enough. The days I spent crying—the endless nights—empty. It's a year.

EVELYN. That's too soon, Rita.

RITA. Only I can decide that, Evelyn. (*Pause.*) You're old-fashioned.

EVELYN. Maybe, but you're crazy to be doing this at all ... After Charlie died, you went wacko ... Took up acting ... You're nearly seventy!

RITA. I only do it as a hobby. I don't want to be a star. What's wrong with doing it for enjoyment?

EVELYN. It's crazy!

RITA. I always wanted to be an actress. (*Pause.*) In high school I played in all the shows ... Oh, you should have seen me ... Then what did I do afterwards? Get married. Isn't that what everybody did then? Take care of a husband, raise children, take care of a house ... be a caretaker ... My dream died ... slowly ... Now my children are grown—my husband is dead ... But I'm alive ... My dream is coming back.

EVELYN. But so are your children this weekend. Don't you think you have a responsibility towards them?

RITA. To them?

EVELYN. Yes, they want to be with you on the anniversary of your husband's death ... And you're going to be prancing around on a stage in *that*.

RITA. I have my own life to lead now.

EVELYN. But they're coming to see you, be with you.

RITA. Yes, but I don't want them to. I don't need them now. I have my own life and they have theirs.

EVELYN. You act like you're disowned or something. They send you things, cheese, baskets of fruits, from time to time. And look at the interest they're showing.

RITA. Yes, now.

EVELYN. In a way, it's more than my children. I don't know why they moved so far away—to Iceland. It's like another planet. If I hear from them twice a year I'm lucky. Sometimes I think my children are senile.

RITA. That may very well be, Evelyn. But it's more than that. Our grown children have gone their own ways.

EVELYN. But your children—

RITA. All I'm saying is that I feel separate from my children now.

EVELYN. What a selfish woman you've become.

RITA. Maybe. But my problem all my life has been that I've been too giving—to everyone—my children, my husband. Now I want time for myself.

EVELYN. But not this weekend. Call up the theater, I mean the loft. Have somebody else do your part. Look, you're not getting any money for it.

RITA. I don't know if I can tell them that.

EVELYN. If you're not taking my advice, Rita, how can I help you?

RITA. You can help me by calling my children.

EVELYN. What?

RITA. Yes, calling them and telling them that you and George will be with me this weekend. If they hear it from you, maybe they'll change their minds.

EVELYN. No, no! I'm not going to lie, especially on the first anniversary of your husband's death.

RITA. Don't be so moralistic, Evelyn. Surely you can do me this favor.

EVELYN. Why don't I call that loft—tell them the situation?

RITA. No, call my children, Evelyn.

EVELYN. I can't.

RITA. For me, for our friendship of twenty-five years.

EVELYN. I just don't want to be involved in this. You'll have to invite them to see the play when they're here.

RITA. But I can't let them see the play. Not that there's anything vulgar about it—there isn't. It's just the idea, Evelyn ... I'm sure they'll be hurt and won't understand.

EVELYN. I don't blame them. They have a right to be. (*Pause.*) No, I won't do it.

RITA. (*Rises, whirling around; British accent.*) I am sixty-eight years young. I eat Barricini chocolates. (*Picks up bubble liquid from table and begins blowing bubbles from the wand in jar.*)

EVELYN. I can't bear it! (*Pause.*)

RITA. What I can't bear is your attitude. After all these years, I find out that I have no friends. (*Pause.*) Not one who comes through when you really need her. (*Pause.*)

EVELYN. I suppose a good friend would do it for another good friend. After all, we've been friends for ages.

RITA. Oh, thank you. I knew you'd come through. Good old Evelyn. I knew I could count on you. (*Pause, then puts wand back in bubble jar and replaces on table.*)

EVELYN. (*Sniffing.*) I never thought you'd come to this, Rita. (*Pause.*) Because I am your real and best friend, I'm going to save you the embarrassment, the shame ... Give me Carolyn's number.

RITA. (*Hands address book to her with page open.*) Here.

EVELYN. (*Reads number, dials, then replaces book on table.*) Your daughter first ... All right ...

(*Pause. RITA hovers over her during the conversation.*)

EVELYN. Hello ... Carolyn ... This is Mrs. Kane ... Evelyn Kane ... Yes, your mother's next-door neighbor ... Yes, I'm fine ... Everything is all right ... Listen, Carolyn ... Your mother doesn't know I'm calling you—but she mentioned you were thinking of coming this weekend ... I mean planning ... yes ... Well,

George and I were going to be with her ... You see, we had it all planned. A visit to the cemetery ... A quiet weekend ... I'm just saying that she won't be alone ... Oh, I see ... Everything is packed? ... It's not necessary, really ... I understand ... The memory of your father is sacred ... And you should all be together at home quietly. (*Begins to sniff.*) Just a cold, Carolyn ... All right. Don't mention my call, please. I hope I see you ... Good-bye. (*SHE hangs up.*) Such a wonderful daughter—you should count your blessings, Rita ...

RITA. A beautiful try, Evelyn, but it failed.

EVELYN. You really should be ashamed of yourself.

RITA. (*Picks up address book, opens it.*) Please try Mark's number now ... Maybe if you could convince him not to come, he can call Carolyn ...

EVELYN. The whole thing is confusing.

RITA. No, please, Evelyn. Finish the job. Here's his number. (*Hands address book to her again.*)

EVELYN. (*Dials the number; long pause.*) No answer ... (*Waits.*)

RITA. Oh, hang up, already. You can try later.

EVELYN. (*Puts phone back on hook.*) No, it's all settled. They're coming. And you're going to be with them.

(*Hands address book back to RITA, who replaces it on table.*)

RITA. (*Sits.*) Who are you to tell me what to do?

EVELYN. How dare you speak to me that way? After doing you that big favor ... By phoning I told a terrible lie.

RITA. Thanks for the favor. Don't worry, you'll still go to heaven even after that terrible lie.

EVELYN. I don't know what's wrong with you. Why don't you stop all this nonsense? First it was the part-time job, when your husband left you so well provided for. But it turned out that even that job wasn't enough.

RITA. It keeps me busy, but it's so unfulfilling. For it's only a job. I want to do something that matters. Why can't a woman do that? How many years do we have left to do what we want? Why dream of what we once wanted? Let's just do it!

EVELYN. Instead of taking up acting, you should take life easy, like George and I. We're happy.

RITA. Sitting like zombies in front of the television set?

EVELYN. We enjoy it.

RITA. When I come to your house and ask him what's happening in the news, he looks at me like I'm crazy. He doesn't know.

EVELYN. The paper and TV make him sleepy.

RITA. It's not a very productive kind of life.

EVELYN. He worked hard all his life. Doesn't he have the right to relax the way he wants to?

RITA. Yes, I suppose he does.

EVELYN. We take vacations—a week or two in the country, take in the sunshine—fresh air—what else is there? When you're old? After a lifetime of working, just breathe the clean air—enjoy the pleasures of retirement.

RITA. It makes me sad to think of the way Charlie killed himself to make a living—working, working, working, no enjoyment ... Always planning for the day when he'd retire. Oh, he had great dreams ... A farm house with a horse or two ... ducks, geese, sheep, chickens ... and we'd sit on the porch ... in the clear air ... But then he died before he had a chance to make it happen ... Ironic, isn't it? But that wasn't my dream ... (*Pause.*) Now it's time for myself. I want to fulfill myself—my own being. (*Pause.*) You can't help it if your life is so ungratifying.

EVELYN. Ungratifying? I go with George for walks. He loves the parks. Even though they're all filthy now and covered with dog-you-know-what. And then he loves to listen to night-time radio talk shows so I stay up and hear him call in and talk. They give him fifteen minutes. George loves to reminisce about the good old days. Then we go to Roseland because we met there and our names are on those plaques on the wall. George loves to see it.

RITA. Why live through him? Everything for him. Do you stop to think of what makes *you* happy? What *you* want to do?

EVELYN. I want to make him happy, so I'll be happy.

RITA. But surely you have interests?

EVELYN. Interests?

RITA. Interests. Things you enjoy doing. Hobbies, pastimes.

EVELYN. Oh, one time I wanted to be an artist. Go to Paris, live a bohemian life. But didn't every woman want to be something at one time?

RITA. Who says you can't paint now?

EVELYN. Now? Paint? Are you crazy?

RITA. You have the time. Just buy the paints.

EVELYN. George is allergic to paints. He sneezes.

RITA. Come and paint in my house.

EVELYN. I can't. My hands are arthritic ... I'm happy with my life, Rita. I'm taking it easy ... What are you trying to stir up?

RITA. I'm just trying to make you realize that you're not fulfilled. You're not doing anything.

EVELYN. There's nothing I want to do.

RITA. So you're going to sit around till you die? (*Pause. Rises.*) Now we have some time. How much, we don't know. That's why we've got to seize it now. Don't let it rush by us. (*SHE begins jogging slowly around the room.*)

EVELYN. Do you think you're having a breakdown?

RITA. No.

EVELYN. I do ... look at you ... and this whole thing about your children and you not wanting to see them ... (*Pause.*) And you do the strangest things lately.

RITA. Like what? (*SHE is now doing simple calisthenics.*)

EVELYN. Like thinking you're an athlete.

RITA. I'm exercising. It's good for me. (*SHE continues exercises.*)

EVELYN. And you even ride a bicycle!

RITA. That's even better exercise, Evelyn.

EVELYN. An old woman on a bicycle?

RITA. I want to keep in shape. I'm sixty-eight years young! (*SHE moves up on toes and stretches her arms in the air.*)

EVELYN. Ha!

RITA. I had to get in shape physically for acting.

EVELYN. And then all those vitamins with that horrible-looking granola. I don't understand it.

RITA. I want to be healthy. It all helped me prepare for the stage. (*SHE does breathing exercises.*)

EVELYN. You're really bit by this acting bug, only it seems to have stung your brain.

RITA. (*Sits down on couch, reflective.*) Do you know the moment I love best? When everybody is seated, the house is dark. And then slowly the lights go up. Like magic time. And it's a whole new world.

EVELYN. But to be at that world at your age—

RITA. I know I can do it now. I want it. (*Pause.*) I remember when Charlie and I used to reminisce about our childhood, to see how far we could remember. He could remember colors, the color of his crib, his pajamas. And do you know what I remembered—pictures in books of ladies with pinafores, gentlemen with high-buttoned shoes, singing, dancing ... And I remembered what I wanted to be ... Once Charlie said, "Do you really think you would have been an actress if you didn't get married, raise a family?"

EVELYN. And what did you say?

RITA. I said, I don't know. How does anybody know? If such and such was—if this was that way—why think about it?—torment yourself about it? I spent the major portion of my life as a housewife. Fifty years.

EVELYN. That's half a century.

RITA. Yes. Half a century of doing for others.

EVELYN. I've put in close to half a century.

RITA. All the years ... They pass so quickly. (*Pause.*) Sometimes I think about the people who grew old with me ... They retired to warm climates, the Southeast, the Southwest ... I get postcards every so often ... The husband with a golf stick in this hand smiling, his wife waving ... surrounded by green grass ... then the ones in mobile homes in the West, living out their lives ... the ones who are dead and buried somewhere.

EVELYN. Yes.

RITA. That's why you have to spend the rest of your life doing what you want. It's my last chance to fulfill the dream of a lifetime. (*Pause.*)

(*EVELYN rises and gently pulls RITA toward the audience, to an "imaginary" mirror.*)

EVELYN. Look in the mirror. What do you see?

RITA. I see a woman—an older woman trying to begin her life again.

EVELYN. No. Let me tell you what I see. An old woman thinking she's sweet sixteen.

RITA. Don't make fun of me. Inside I still feel sweet sixteen. (*Moves around the room.*)

EVELYN. Rita, I know you for twenty-five years. I know what's good for you. This isn't. (*Pause.*) What you need is a man.

RITA. No. Men are not my answer right now.

EVELYN. You joined a women's lib group? I heard they have them for old women now.

RITA. I have not joined a women's lib group. I've come to my senses—my feelings.

EVELYN. But isn't it lonely without a steady man around? Admit it.

RITA. Sometimes, but I've gone with other men since Charlie died. To this social, that social. They talk about their security, their pensions, their men's clubs—when they chased bears down mountains—

EVELYN. (*Sits on couch.*) You don't want to give to them. You're shut off in your own world.

RITA. Evelyn, maybe you should go back to your apartment. You're making me nervous.

EVELYN. Well, George is reading the newspaper and watching TV. He doesn't talk much when he does that.

RITA. So why don't you start to do something? For yourself ... You always said you liked working with your hands.

EVELYN. My hands?

RITA. Yes.

EVELYN. I always did like working with my hands. (*Rises and begins arranging Rita's flower bowl on table.*)

RITA. You always arrange them so well. Flower arranging is an art. Maybe you should start doing that.

EVELYN. Oh, look, Rita. I'm not about to start anything now. I don't think much of this old age. It's something that happens. You get pains, here and there, this hurts, that hurts. You don't know when it's going to be over ... (*Sits on couch.*)

RITA. We have opportunities, but you don't see them. Look how long we've lived. We have knowledge, wisdom, those things youth can never have ... You make us sound like we're all invalids to be cast aside. We have strengths.

EVELYN. Strengths. What strengths?

(*Pause.*)

RITA. (*Sits on couch.*) I'll tell you a story about strength. A ninety-year-old woman learned wood carving.

EVELYN. Ninety years old? She should be resting at her age.

RITA. According to you. Evelyn, that woman is alive and so are we!

EVELYN. Alive?

RITA. Yes, alive! ... Why does everybody think of old age as a time to freeze—a time to die? ... to be dumped like scrap iron? ... People in beds, motionless, waiting for their eyes to finally close ... No, this is a time for our freedom.

EVELYN. Those vitamins you take must have dope in them.

RITA. You should take some. (*Rises, picks up vitamin bottle from table and shakes it at Evelyn.*) They'll pep you up.

EVELYN. Vitamins at my age? I've never taken any. No reason to start now.

RITA. (*Puts down vitamin bottle.*) That's your problem. Your whole life is set. A routine, the same pattern, it never changes. Never try anything new—even if it's a small thing like a vitamin. (*Pause. SHE sits.*)

EVELYN. I can't wait for your children to get here and pull you back to your senses.

RITA. I'm fine. I'm just trying to get through to you. (*Pause.*) Sometimes I see you walking with George. Following him. You go where he goes.

EVELYN. So?

RITA. So? Can't you understand? Don't you want to explore for yourself?

EVELYN. Explore, Rita? Please! This conversation is going in circles. I'm getting dizzy. (*Pause*.) Why not forget about this play? Why don't we go out tonight? Look, we'll have a good time ... I'll drag him away from the paper and the TV. We'll have dinner and then go to Roseland. (*Pause*.) We'll have fun, a lot of laughs. George is a riot when he wants to be. When he talks about the way the streets used to be paved ... a place where he used to work where waiters sang and danced Irish jigs ...

RITA. What do you remember, Evelyn?

EVELYN. Me?

RITA. Yes.

EVELYN. (*Pause*.) Well, I never gave it much thought, but ... let's see ... (*Pause*.) On every Sunday in June, oh, it was years ago, they were such bright Sundays ... there would be lots of cars going by ... They had posters which said, "Just Married." And old beat-up shoes and tin cans were tied to the cars. And the tin cans made so much noise as they rode along. I think all the young women picked a Sunday in June to get married ... (*Pause*.) Come on, Rita, we'll all go out and reminisce ...

RITA. No, I can't ... I want to go over the script again.

EVELYN. So you really intend to go through with it? Not caring about anyone but yourself? (*Pause*.) Did you ever stop to think that you're about to make a fool of yourself?

RITA. A fool of myself?

EVELYN. Yes. Your first time on the stage in over forty years—no, fifty years, right? It's been ages.

RITA. Yes, but I'm confident that everything will be all right. Nothing will happen.

EVELYN. What if you forget your lines?

RITA. My part is mostly pantomime.

EVELYN. How will it feel to be the laughingstock in front of a lot of people?

RITA. Why should I be the laughingstock?

EVELYN. I can just hear everybody asking, who does she think she is, somebody so old thinking they can act and wearing that leotard ... Let's face it, your figure isn't what it used to be.

RITA. That may be true. But people aren't that cruel. I'm old, but I'm still a person and deserve to be treated with respect.

EVELYN. The way old people are treated? They're laughed at or pitied.

RITA. No, Evelyn.

EVELYN. Yes, Rita. I'm telling you for your own good. Come on, take that off. Put on a dress. Throw away that script. (*Pause.*) Besides, you were probably cast because that director felt sorry for you.

RITA. No, the director liked me very much. He said, "For a woman your age, you certainly have a magnetism."

EVELYN. He probably felt sorry for you. Like people giving old people seats on trains and buses, they feel sorry for them, because they feel they might die any second.

RITA. Why do you think he pitied me?

EVELYN. Well, it just seems funny to me that he'd pick someone with no experience for the part. He's not paying you, is he?

RITA. No, as a matter of fact I offered to make a contribution to the theater group for ... (*SHE stops, she has slipped.*)

EVELYN. Now I see everything, old girl!

RITA. I don't know what you're talking about!

EVELYN. Come on, Rita. I'm not a fool and neither are you.

RITA. (*Stands and moves away.*) I won't listen to your nonsense, Evelyn. My small donation to the theater was only—only a gesture—a gesture of good will.

EVELYN. Well, I'm sure it meant a great deal. Those crazy theaters have nothing. They were probably very grateful for your "good will." Face it, Rita. They needed your money.

RITA. (*After a long moment.*) Maybe you're right. Give the old hag a chance, he thought, out of pity, sadness ... out of a need for my money.

EVELYN. (*Rises and goes to her.*) You finally see the light.

RITA. The cast probably talked about me. Who's that crazy old woman? (*SHE takes the script from table and throws it on the floor.*)

EVELYN. That's where it belongs.

RITA. Take a look at me! You're right. The audience will howl.

(*Puts her caftan back on; EVELYN helps her.*)

RITA. Every audition I've gone to they've all been young. I stuck out like a sore thumb. Old women don't take up acting.

EVELYN. Oh, honey, don't torment yourself now.

RITA. He cast me for the money, Evelyn. I've been such a fool. (*Sinks onto couch.*)

EVELYN. (*Sits beside her.*) Oh, Rita, just think of having a good time tonight. Look, I've got to start talking George into—

RITA. Going? Dragging him away from his routine?

EVELYN. Oh, he'll love it. He likes you. He'll be glad!

RITA. He hardly says a word to me. Just nods.

EVELYN. George is a wonderful dancer.

RITA. He never dances. Just stands around looking into space as though he were remembering something he lost fifty years ago.

EVELYN. Come on, don't take it out on George. Think of the great time we'll all have tonight. In a few days, the mourning begins, silence ... remembrance ... with your children.

RITA. Yes ... You're right ...

EVELYN. At last you've come around to my way of thinking. I knew I could talk some sense into you. Well, I'm going to give George a buzz. (*Dials phone.*) Hello ... George ... Yes, Evelyn, who else? George, let's all go to Roseland tonight with Rita ... All three of us ... It'll be such fun ...

Her children are coming this weekend ... Yes, her children ... Carolyn and Mark ... To commemorate Charlie's death ... Charlie ... her husband ... Dead one year ... They'll all be staying at home ... to be with her ... So I thought why not go out tonight ... a few days before ... cheer her up a bit ... It'll be so much fun ... Oh, don't be that way ... Think of the good time we'll all have ... Oh, all right ... Look, when Carolyn and Mark come ... Rita's children ... Carolyn and Mark ... we'll all get together for coffee and discuss things—current events. (*Slowly hangs up.*) He's watching the news and reading the paper. I suppose I should be in there with him. I don't know why I'm here so long ... I suppose it's because he's reading the news and watching TV.

RITA. I don't know why he watches the news and reads the paper at the same time. He just stares at them both ... like sleeping with his eyes open.

EVELYN. I know. He doesn't want to go to Roseland tonight but maybe some other night, Rita?

RITA. We'll see.

EVELYN. Oh, I wish you'd say yes. You wanted to tonight. You were so excited. Look, we'll make it up to you. (*Pause.*) I better go in now ... Or he gets mad ... He doesn't talk to me as it is ... Oh, well ... You know how men are ... But he was excited to hear that your children were coming. And he thought it was only proper that you spend the weekend quietly with them.

RITA. Did he say that?

EVELYN. Well, not exactly in those words, but he meant it, anyway ... He thinks it's only right for them to be with you on that sacred occasion.

RITA. I got the feeling that he didn't know who my children were. You had to keep repeating their names.

EVELYN. Oh, no. He knew who they were. Well, when Carolyn and Mark come we'll all get together ... it'll be nice ...

RITA. (*Rises and crosses down to "imaginary" mirror.*) I don't know how much time I'll have ... My time is so limited this weekend.

EVELYN. (*Rises.*) But you won't be in the play ...

RITA. I don't know ...

EVELYN. (*Moving down to her.*) Rita, this get-together with your children on this sacred occasion is the only thing that matters this weekend ... Don't you want to share Charlie's memory with them? Think of what it's going to feel like to be with them again.

RITA. Yes ... talking quietly about all the good times we had with Charlie ... We'll all hold each other tight ...

EVELYN. Tears of joy are beginning, Rita.

RITA. But then what? What about all the silences? So much distance and time between us...

EVELYN. But this weekend you'll be reunited!

RITA. Yes, I guess we will be.

EVELYN. That's the way it should be. (*Moves from "imaginary" mirror.*) What kind of mother thinks only of herself?

RITA. I suppose my time should be theirs this weekend. (*Pause.*) So my life has to stop for them.

EVELYN. You act like it's the end of the world. You have nothing to do.

RITA. How can you say that? I have something important to do, something very important to me ...

EVELYN. Are you still talking about that play? You're not going on in that play ...

RITA. (*Suddenly picking up script from floor.*) Yes! Yes, I am! (*Takes off caftan, drapes it over corner of couch again.*) I guess I let all the old fears take over! I was cast because the director thought *I could do it.* He believed in me ...

EVELYN. But what you said before—?

RITA. You were forcing me to say it! It doesn't matter *how* I got the part. The most important thing is that *I can handle it.*

EVELYN. But what about your children?

RITA. (*Pause.*) I won't tell them about the play.

EVELYN. (*Sits on couch.*) Thank God for that.

RITA. When they call I'll just tell them that I'm going to be busy this weekend. But there'll be time for us to go to the cemetery. Put flowers on his grave. Lilacs. Charlie loved lilacs.

EVELYN. That's the least you could do.

RITA. (*moving around room.*) And we'll all cry ... He really was a wonderful man. I think he'd be happy to know that I was acting in a play. (*Pause.*) And then on with the course of living ... We'll all have lunch ... Then the rest of the time is my own.

EVELYN. (*Rises and goes to Rita.*) Think it over. You may lose your children forever. If they find out, they won't forgive you.

RITA. You might be right. But how can I hide it? I guess I'll have to find the courage to tell them and pray they understand.

EVELYN. (*Pause.*) Well, I've tried my best. (*SHE is about to start out.*) Good luck, Rita, you'll need it!

RITA. Thanks, Evelyn.

(*But EVELYN lingers on, looks at the flowers and then rearranges one or two.*)

RITA. That looks nice.

EVELYN. I guess I *do* have a knack with my hands.

RITA. Yes, you do.

EVELYN. Crazy at this age to have a knack with your hands. Oh well, what are you going to do? I've got to go in and watch the news with him.

RITA. And I guess I'll practice my part. (*Pause.*) You will come to the play, won't you, Evelyn?

EVELYN. Rita, I wouldn't miss it for the world!

(*THEY hug warmly.*)

BLACKOUT

Costume Plot

RITA: Full-length caftan or robe

                         Flesh color leotard with
                              matching tights
                              worn underneath
                              caftan or robe (or it
                              can be a costume
                              that's equally
                              outrageous worn
                              underneath caftan
                              or robe).
                         Casual shoes

EVELYN: Plain housedress
                         House slippers or casual
                              shoes
                         Hosiery
                         Wedding band

PROPERTY PLOT

Set Pieces:	Couch (could be formed by row of chairs with material draped over them).
	Two end tables
Props (Pre-set):	On Table "A" Telephone (doesn't have to be a working one) Address book (beside phone) Plastic jar of bubble liquid containing wand Bottle of vitamins Playscript (in manuscript form)
	On Table "B" Flowers in bowl (or vase) (can be artificial) Small framed photograph of man, "Charlie."
Optional:	Set dressing on walls (if any): Old movie posters Family photographs Theatrical memorabilia

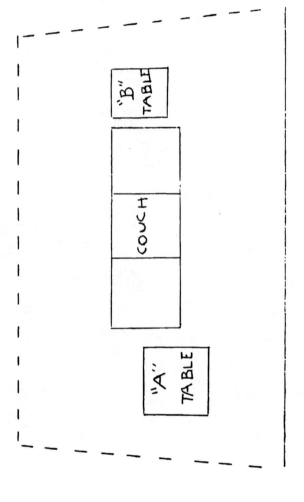

GROUND PLAN FOR "SECOND CHANCE"

"B" TABLE

COUCH

"A" TABLE

(NOTE: ENTRANCE CAN BE STAGE RIGHT, STAGE LEFT, OR UP CENTER.)

ADMIT ONE

Admit One was presented in the Playwrights/ Directors Unit of The Actors Studio in New York City in 1983, under the direction of Fred Sadoff, with the following cast:

HAROLD CONKLIN............................ Mike Kellin
MEGAN MATTHEWS..........................Sally Moffet

A subsequent production was staged by The Barn Players' Senior Acting Program in Overland Park, Kansas.

CHARACTERS

HAROLD CONKLIN   a feisty seventy-five in
                         good shape; has a
                         certain charm.

MEGAN MATTHEWS   fifty-nine, attractive
                         but shy.

TIME

The present. An afternoon of a June day.

PLACE

A room in a modest, but respectable hotel in midtown
Manhattan.

ADMIT ONE

SCENE: A small hotel room. There is one bed and a nightstand. On the nightstand are a radio and lamp. There is a bureau (or a table). On the top of the bureau are a paper bag, containing two full wine bottles, two small plastic glasses and a stack of letters. Two chairs are also in the room.

(If there are walls, there is a picture hanging crookedly, a window, and a mirror over the bureau. If there are no walls, the actors pantomime any action regarding these objects.)

AT RISE: HAROLD, looking very dapper, is admiring himself in a mirror. HE straightens his tie, then HE looks at the crooked picture on the wall. KNOCKING on door.

HAROLD. Just a minute! *(HE tries to straighten crooked picture but it doesn't budge.)* Coming!

(HE races to door, then stops short, hesitates for a minute and finally opens it. MEGAN, who is dressed tastefully, stand there, looking very hesitant.)

HAROLD. Well, come on in.

(*SHE does not move.*)

HAROLD. Aren't you going to come in?

(*SHE is silent.*)

HAROLD. You okay?
MEGAN. I think so.
HAROLD. Please come in.

(*SHE walks into the room, slowly.*)

HAROLD. Well, sit down. Anywhere you like.
MEGAN. (*Sits down in chair.*) There, I've seated myself. (*Pause.*) I'm a bit nervous.
HAROLD. So am I. (*Pause, extends his hand.*) Well, I'm Harold Conklin. You can call me Hal.
MEGAN. Nice to meet you, Harold. (*Pause.*) I'm Megan Matthews.
HAROLD. I know. (*Pause.*) You know, your name rhymes in a way ... Did anyone ever tell you that?
MEGAN. Some people.

(*Silence.*)

HAROLD. (*Moving to bureau.*) Something to drink? Red or white wine?
MEGAN. I don't drink.

HAROLD. I don't drink myself ... I used to a long time ago ... (*Pause.*) But I bought some wine just for the occasion. (*HE takes out two bottles from paper bag and twists off their tops.*) Well, I'll have me some red wine ... red wine is good for the blood ... I want you to know that nothing's wrong with my blood ... But it's healthier to drink red wine ... Now, what do you want?

MEGAN. I told you that I don't drink.

HAROLD. You don't drink nothing?

MEGAN. I drink tea.

HAROLD. Well, I don't have a kitchen to make you some. Sorry, I didn't think I needed a kitchen. I only rented this room to meet everyone. (*Pause.*) How long did it take you to get here?

MEGAN. Oh, about forty minutes.

HAROLD. You say you're from Flushing?

MEGAN. Yes, and it took me about forty minutes from Flushing.

HAROLD. That's not bad ... (*Pause.*) It's damn good ... You made very good time, Megan.

MEGAN. So I did.

(*Pause.*)

HAROLD. It would have taken you a helluva lot longer if you came out to Long Island ... It would have cost you a lot more ... more in time and money ... It's just easier to do it this way ...

MEGAN. You're a very thoughtful man, taking this room. You saved me a big trip.

HAROLD. Well, I think of other people. (*Pause.*) Women like that, don't they?

MEGAN. I guess so.

HAROLD. (*Has poured himself a glass of wine and takes a drink.*) You know, you're just like I thought you'd be ...

MEGAN. How's that?

HAROLD. (*Sits on other chair.*) Soft like your voice on the phone ... Did you picture me to look like this?

MEGAN. A little ... but I thought you might be heavier ...

HAROLD. Me, heavy, nah ... just solid ... Do you want to feel a solid stomach?

MEGAN. No, thank you. I believe you. (*Gets up, walks around the room, looks at picture.*) You know, that picture is crooked.

HAROLD. I know. I tried to straighten it out before ... no luck.

MEGAN. (*Looks at it again.*) Just a cluster of clouds—drifting.

HAROLD. Yeah, drifting along.

MEGAN. It's not a very good picture of clouds.

HAROLD. I told you it's just a room. And I'm no moneybags ... In my day, a room like this was a dollar. You wouldn't believe what they get for this now ...

MEGAN. I can imagine. (*Pause; walks to window.*) Not much of a view ... just a brick wall

... (*Walking around again.*) Not much in here ... Why don't they put up a shelf with a few books?

HAROLD. (*Gestures toward nightstand.*) Just the holy Bible. Amen.

MEGAN. Why do they put Bibles in hotel rooms?

HAROLD. Hotels are damn depressing ... so when somebody thinks of jumping out the window ... they can read the Bible ... The Bible has saved a lot of lives. (*After a few sips, HE rises and sets down glass on bureau.*)

MEGAN. Is that so?

HAROLD. Hey, you're so serious ... Why don't you relax?

(*Pause.*)

MEGAN. (*Looking at her watch.*) What time do you have? My watch is slow.

HAROLD. Why do you want to check the time? You got somewhere else to go?

MEGAN. Well ...

HAROLD. You do?

MEGAN. No.

HAROLD. Why are you so jumpy? You being followed or something? Hey, you're not wanted for anything?

MEGAN. I don't think so. (*Pause.*) You still didn't tell me the time.

HAROLD. (*Looks at his watch.*) It's a little after four.

MEGAN. (*Looks at her watch.*) Oh ... I am slow.

HAROLD. It didn't get dark ... if that's what you're thinking.

MEGAN. Very witty.

HAROLD. (*Pause.*) Yeah.

MEGAN. I liked your ad.

HAROLD. Thanks.

MEGAN. It was direct, to the point. (*Pause.*) And easy to remember. "Mature gentleman has own home near beach. In good health and active. Seeks sincere lady 45-60 for love and marriage. Must enjoy living, fishing, travel, etc."

HAROLD. It took me a long time to think of it ... You know, it was hard for me to get the right words ... I didn't know if I wanted a picture too. Then I thought, you women would think it was a lot of trouble and then I would get pictures from twenty-five years ago.

MEGAN. I think it worked without the picture.

HAROLD. It was okay.

MEGAN. May I ask you a question?

HAROLD. Go right ahead.

MEGAN. (*Sits in her previous chair.*) Why did you put in an ad?

HAROLD. Because I couldn't meet a woman.

MEGAN. This city is packed with women searching for men—especially older women.

HAROLD. I know. But they're old fuddy-duddies or they want a meal-ticket. And from the letters I got, *these* women don't seem much better. (*Moves toward bureau.*)

MEGAN. How many letters did you get?

HAROLD. About fifty and they're still coming in. Called the newspaper today ... and they said there's another ten ... So that'll make sixty ... (*He picks up stack of letters.*)

MEGAN. Amazing!

HAROLD. (*Waving the stack.*) See?

MEGAN. A multitude of letters ...

HAROLD. I didn't expect so many.

MEGAN. What were they like?

HAROLD. The letters?

MEGAN. No, the women who wrote them.

HAROLD. (*During this HE replaces the stack on bureau.*) I didn't meet most of them. A lot of them sounded like duds and weirdos. I got that from over the phone. You see, I screened them out first ... One woman was into causes like saving the whales. She was looking for someone to go around demonstrating with her ... to raise hell with her ... Another was looking for me to support her grandchildren ... Another wanted to have a baby ... Now, mind you, she was sixty-five ... Then there was a sex change too ... and a vegetarian who was a lush ... Boy, I heard plenty over that telephone ... a lot of strange women out there!

MEGAN. But of the women you met?

HAROLD. (*Sits on edge of bed.*) I met four. One of them I took out for dinner. You know, she got a doggy-bag for her leftovers and *mine* too. She said that these leftovers would last her two meals ... Boy, she was so happy—grinning like crazy at the doggy-bag ... That's all she was interested in ... I'll tell you there wasn't too much left on my plate ... but that didn't stop her.

MEGAN. How sad!

HAROLD. When I didn't order dessert, that made her mad as hell.

MEGAN. What about the other three women? Did you like them?

HAROLD. (*Rises, pulls out her letter from inside his jacket.*) Look, what's the difference ... Now you're the fifth ... I liked your letter ... You wrote in on pink stationery ... It has such a nice smell. You sounded so nice on the phone.

MEGAN. Are you disappointed?

HAROLD. No ... I like the way you look. You look very nice ... What do you think of me?

MEGAN. Excuse me, I don't feel too well. There is a bathroom?

HAROLD. (*Pointing.*) It's that way.

(*SHE hurriedly exits to bathroom and HE mutters to himself, tucking away her letter, inside his jacket.*)

HAROLD. Why did this happen to me? Nobody else threw up ... And I thought I was good-looking for my age ... I guess she doesn't think so.

MEGAN. (*Re-enters.*) I'm very sorry.

HAROLD. Are you okay now?

MEGAN. My stomach was just a little bit upset ... I'm fine now.

HAROLD. Am I that bad to look at?

MEGAN. It's not you ... It's me ... You look fine. You're a nice-looking man.

HAROLD. You're saying that to make me feel good. Can't be Clark Gable at seventy-five?

MEGAN. You're seventy-five? You don't look it.

HAROLD. Well, thanks.

MEGAN. I can't believe you're seventy-five.

HAROLD. Why? You got something against someone my age?

MEGAN. No .,. Quite the contrary, I find it fascinating. (*SHE sits on chair.*)

HAROLD. Because I'm on old-timer. (*Pause.*) I bet you never saw horses going down the streets.

MEGAN. Not really.

HAROLD. In the early 1900's, it was horses mostly. If the kids would see a car, they'd yell, "Get a horse."

MEGAN. Charming.

HAROLD. (*Moving about.*) Going back, you know, I liked when everything was a nickel. A loaf of bread, ice cream, the 6th Avenue El ... and the *Nickelette* was five cents ... You could see a double feature for a nickel ... Now a nickel's not worth a damn ... (*Pause, turns to her.*) Hey, how do you feel?

MEGAN. My stomach feels better already ... My stomach was upset before ... Nerves, you know ... This is a new experience ... But I'm enjoying it.

HAROLD. Every time I do this ... I get the jitters ... but I haven't thrown up yet ... but I do get shaky ... I don't know how young kids do it ... I mean, they started this kind of thing with the personals.

MEGAN. I think it took a lot of courage to place an ad in a newspaper.

HAROLD. Loneliness makes you do things you'd be embarrassed to even think about. (*Pause. HE sits again on edge of bed.*) Why don't we get started?

MEGAN. What do you mean?

HAROLD. I mean getting to know you. I'll ask you the questions. Now, you told me you were a good cook.

MEGAN. Yes, I am.

HAROLD. What are your specialties?

MEGAN. Chicken—all kinds of chicken—potted, broiled, roasted, chicken with lemon, orange, pineapple, chicken stuffed with ham and cheese or stuffed with raisins and walnuts ...

HAROLD. I'm getting hungry. Now, that's the one thing I'm so damn bad at ... cooking ... Now whoever I end up with, I'll take out twice a week ... I want to take my wife out ... I don't want to have her cook all the time ... Both my wives were great cooks.

MEGAN. You were married twice?

HAROLD. When I was twenty-two—that lasted till I was forty-five. Then I got married at fifty and that lasted till I was seventy ... Both my wives died. Had no children from of any of them.

(*Pause.*) Now, you said in your letter you never married.

MEGAN. No, I never married.

HAROLD. Well, I want you to know that ... out of the whole batch of letters you were the only one who was single.

MEGAN. I guess I'm a rarity. Today women don't get married that often ... In my day, everyone did ... I must be some kind of freak to you, Mr. Conklin.

HAROLD. Now, I wouldn't say something like that ... But why didn't you get married? I bet you got lots of offers.

MEGAN. I did. But I had to turn down all my offers. You see, it was because of my parents. They were always sick ... in bad health ... I had to take care of them ... I felt it was my obligation ... so I had to devote my life to them.

HAROLD. What a shame!

MEGAN. Please don't pity me, Mr. Conklin. Actually it's a very heroic thing when a child takes care of her parents ... It's a very brave feat ... It's very virtuous ... Neighbors, relatives and friends have said, "Katherine and Michael's girl was always there for her parents." I had the patience of a saint, Mr. Conklin. I'm a religious hero.

HAROLD. Heroes are made in wars.

MEGAN. That's sarcastic ... sardonic.

HAROLD. Talk English, woman.

MEGAN. You don't know what those words mean?

HAROLD. I was never big on school ... I know you've been a schoolteacher ... But I never finished high school ... I was a damn rebel ... busy with girls and bikes.

MEGAN. You neglected your studies?

HAROLD. Yep ... I was "Hal, the Hell-Raiser." Racing down those streets on my bike, everyone got out of my way ...

MEGAN. Do you regret having left school so young?

HAROLD. Nah ... (*Pause.*) How old are you, Megan?

MEGAN. I told you I was forty-nine.

HAROLD. (*Not believing.*) Forty-nine?

MEGAN. You act like I'm lying.

HAROLD. No ... no ... Now, you said you work part-time in your house, reading books. What kind of job is that?

MEGAN. I said *proofreading* books. I check the galleys of books for punctuation, grammar, etc., before they're published.

HAROLD. I never heard of a job like that.

MEGAN. It's a job, believe me ... I used to be a teacher ... But I haven't taught in years.

HAROLD. How come?

MEGAN. Having to take care of my parents ... took all my time ... It drained me ... I had no time or energy left to teach ... I must admit that I loved shaping young minds ... but between my parents and my students, it was too exhausting ... I developed stomach problems—headaches ... After fourteen years, I took a leave of absence and never went back ... I got disability for a while ... I lived on savings ...

HAROLD. Your folks, they're not alive, are they? (*Silence.*) I got no provisions for old parents, children or pets ...

MEGAN. I understand.

HAROLD. Well, they're not living, are they?

(*Silence.*)

MEGAN. No, of course not, they're dead. Why do you think I came here? ... Only because they're dead. You see, in a way, I'm free to do as I wish ... I could never do the things I wanted with them around. Most of my time was for them. Now I can do what I want.

HAROLD. You kept their apartment?

MEGAN. Yes ... Now I'm alone there ... Somehow I can't get used to it. I don't like to be alone ... You understand?

HAROLD. I sure can. (*Pause. HE rises and sits on other chair.*) Well, let's get on with this ... How's your health now? Are you in good shape? I mean, do you get those stomach things a lot? And what about headaches?

MEGAN. I've had no headaches for years. I just got sick today ... Just this once. I'm really in good shape.

HAROLD. (*Thumping his chest.*) Look at my chest ... like Tarzan ... I go bowling ... Oh, my rheumatism acts up now and then ... but I'm in great shape ... Haven't been to a doctor in twenty years.

MEGAN. Neither have I.

HAROLD. We have something in common.

MEGAN. So we do ... I don't get sick anymore. You see, I have no vices. I don't drink, smoke ...

HAROLD. You don't smoke?

MEGAN. No.

HAROLD. Now, you're the first woman I met who doesn't smoke.

MEGAN. And I'm the first woman who was never married.

HAROLD. Yeah ... good combination.

MEGAN. No, I don't smoke, drink, gamble, swear ... I'm totally pure—devoid of any vices. (*Pause.*)

HAROLD. Now, Megan. I've got to ask you something real personal ... You were never married. What about—?

MEGAN. I've had "relationships" with men. My last lover—he was an avid reader. We read books all the time: Jules Verne, Robert Louis Stevenson, Isak Dinesen ...

HAROLD. All you two did was read books? Ha!

MEGAN. (*Annoyed.*) And may I ask *you* something personal?

HAROLD. Yes.

MEGAN. Can you still ...?

HAROLD. Yes, I can ... but not as much as I could when I was younger ...

MEGAN. Frequency doesn't matter ... Sometimes one can just hold another person and that would suffice. (*Pause.*) Lately, I go to sleep with my arms around myself.

HAROLD. Hey, that's no good for you. You could twist yourself into a funny shape.

MEGAN. Then I would need an osteopath.

HAROLD. Who?

MEGAN. Never mind. (*Pause.*) My arms wrapped around me feel good.

HAROLD. Well, you have nothing to worry about with me. I'm still in the running.

(*Silence. HE rises.*)

MEGAN. You know, I still feel strange. I have the same feeling that I had when I came here.

HAROLD. Oh, no. You're not going to—

MEGAN. No ... I just feel uneasy ... I feel like I'm being interviewed for a job.

HAROLD. Well, you just did a little interviewing yourself.

MEGAN. I think I had a right to. (*Pause.*) I guess it's the questions back and forth.

HAROLD. Do you think I like doing this? Sitting and asking questions ... It takes a lot out of you ... I'm a little tired myself. You might say that I'm in a rush ... When you're seventy-five, you gotta move ... I'm getting up there.

MEGAN. Aren't we all?

HAROLD. I still have a few years on you, Megan ... Now I don't know how many I have left ... I'm in a rush to spend them with somebody ... I promised myself I'd get a wife when I was seventy-five ... I'm so damn lonely.

MEGAN. I understand.

HAROLD. But I try to keep busy with my clubs ... but then I go back to an empty house.

MEGAN. What clubs do you belong to?

HAROLD. (*Moving around.*) I'm President of the local Elks Club ... How's that for starters? I'm Vice-President of The Wilderness Walking Club, Secretary of the Friends of Fishing Club. And what clubs do you belong to?

MEGAN. I go to a scrabble club once a week ... and to a book discussion club.

HAROLD. Doesn't sound like there's much action there ... more action in my folk dance group.

MEGAN. Well, you wouldn't be interested in literary clubs.

HAROLD. And you wouldn't be interested where you have to move around, take some action.

MEGAN. I beg your pardon. Maybe my life is sedentary but I can go fishing ... walking ... I can dance, too ...

HAROLD. But you don't ...

MEGAN. I can if I want to.

HAROLD. What's the difference? We both go to different clubs. We do different things. But we're both alone. (*Pause.*) Here's a picture of my house. (*Opens his wallet and takes out photo, leans over her shoulder.*)

MEGAN. It's very nice. I always loved a white house with a backyard and a white picket fence.

HAROLD. And two chaise lounges.

MEGAN. That's nice.

HAROLD. Well, that's the outside. (*Shows another photo.*) Now, here's the inside.

MEGAN. It has an old-fashioned quality which I admire ... Mahogany furniture ... lace curtains ...

HAROLD. The lace curtains are beige.

MEGAN. I see. (*Pause.*) A nice mahogany table ... with doilies ... Dark wood coffee table. Old wall clock.

HAROLD. And those are Oriental carpets.

MEGAN. So I see. It's all very nice.

HAROLD. Both my wives loved this house ... and the best part is that it's all paid up ... And it's one block from the beach ... Do you like the beach? (*Puts photos back in wallet, and wallet back in pocket.*)

MEGAN. Yes.

HAROLD. I think Long Beach is one of the most beautiful beaches in the world. (*Pause.*) When you stand on the porch, you can smell the sea ... (*Pause.*) How about travelling? Have you travelled?

MEGAN. Only to parts of New Jersey.

HAROLD. You know, I've been practically all over the world.

MEGAN. How did you manage that?

HAROLD. Years ago, I worked for this freighter line ... I was a bo'sun.

MEGAN. Oh, that's short for boatswain.

HAROLD. Well, I had charge of the men ... I went to places like Brazil, Venezuela, Africa, Hong Kong ...

MEGAN. How exciting! Which place did you like best?

HAROLD. Brazil ... I loved the people and the beaches ... just as nice as Long Beach.

MEGAN. You must have had a lot of adventures.

HAROLD. (*Sits on edge of bed.*) Yeah, a lot of men would go haywire on ship ... One guy was always seeing mermaids or sea serpents ... And one time, a captain jumped overboard ...

MEGAN. How strange.

HAROLD. The sea does crazy things to men. (*Pause.*) I'll never forget one guy who thought he was Christopher Columbus and he wanted to do all the sailing ... He gave us a hard time so we had to put him in irons.

MEGAN. Really?

HAROLD. Yeah ...

MEGAN. What else did you encounter?

HAROLD. One there was a goddam octopus on the bow of the ship ... It was slowing us down ... That thing wouldn't budge ... So we had to chop it off with an ax.

MEGAN. Weren't you afraid?

HAROLD. Nah ... We were always in some kind of danger ... Lots of time, I ran into tarantulas, snakes ... They never got me ...

MEGAN. Oh ... my ...!

HAROLD. There was always something scary going on ... Once we were near mutiny ... Another time, we ran into typhoons in the South Seas ... but we didn't go down ...

MEGAN. Thank heavens for that! But if you did, I bet you're a good swimmer.

HAROLD. I can't swim.

MEGAN. I don't believe you.

HAROLD. It's true. Most of the men out at sea can't swim to save their lives. But it doesn't matter. In the rough waters, you're a goner, anyway ... But I'll tell you what I did learn to do well, play a mean game of poker and eat like a hog ... Those were the days ... but then it got to be too much ... the booze, boy did I drink! ... I was even putting whiskey in my cereal ... and then the women ... One day it just got to me, Megan ... My marriage was almost ruined account of me being away so much ... So I got a job on shore as a ship inspector ... And then I retired at sixty-five.

MEGAN. So that's your story.

HAROLD. (*Rises, moves around.*) Yep ... Now let me give you the rest of the details. Now, I told you the house is all paid up ... I have a little savings in the bank, a few thousand. I know it's not much ... but I get eight hundred dollars a month ... Now, the house is all yours when I go ... and anything else that's left ... I mean, you have a few years over me.

MEGAN. It's thoughtful to offer your possessions.

HAROLD. Well, it's part of this deal. And there'll be a written agreement with a lawyer.

MEGAN. You have the whole thing planned out?

HAROLD. You can't go into something like this ... without figuring out all the details ... I know I'm offering a damn good life to someone. What man my age could do the same?

MEGAN. I don't mean to sound snide or ungrateful. But you keep talking about what *you're* offering. You never once asked me what kind of life I'm looking for. I'd like you to be aware of my needs. (*Rises.*)

HAROLD. (*Stunned.*) What do you want?

MEGAN. I want a simple life ... I'm basically a homebody ... But I would like to go out once a week to the city, see a play, a foreign film ...

HAROLD. That's okay by me.

MEGAN. As far as your house is concerned—

HAROLD. What about my house?

MEGAN. The furnishings are fine ... But on the dark wood coffee-table, I would like to have a bowl filled with hazel nuts ... and let me see ... teacups with tulips on them.

HAROLD. Well, you want to add a few touches of your own ... That's okay ... I think there's pictures of butterflies on the teacups ... butterflies and maybe a few moths ... Tulips would be nice ... I could use a new set.

MEGAN. And what about your front door?

HAROLD. My front door?

MEGAN. Yes ... Is there a doorbell?

HAROLD. You ring a buzzer on the front door.

MEGAN. I would like a chiming doorbell.

HAROLD. A chiming doorbell?

MEGAN. It's quaint.

HAROLD. Well, we'll see about that ... (*Pause.*) Hey, are you sure you don't want to redo my house?

MEGAN. No ... just these small touches would make all the difference in the world ... Those are my needs. I'm not asking for minks, diamonds, credit cards ... I like to be surrounded by quaintness ...

HAROLD. We'll see ... about that chiming doorbell.

MEGAN. (*Pause.*) Of course, you'll see. It's so silly of me to make these demands. You haven't decided yet ... You can have your pick of women. (*Pause.*) Do you feel powerful ... Herculean?

HAROLD. I don't know if I feel powerful ... I never thought of it that way. But you're right, I should. After all, it's *my* ad.

MEGAN. You're on an ego trip.

HAROLD. (*Doesn't understand the phrase.*) What?

MEGAN. You must be thinking that all these women are at your beck and call. *You* call the shots, Mr. Conklin.

HAROLD. Then put in your own goddam ad... You can do your own picking!

MEGAN. I don't have your nerve.

HAROLD. Now you're starting to give me a hard time.

MEGAN. I'm sorry. You've been so nice.

HAROLD. Because there's something nice about you ... not like the others ... One of them had teased up hair, way up to this ceiling ... And with a mouth that I just wanted to close up like a zipper... In spite of your complaining, they don't make women like you anymore ... You don't smoke or drink ... You took care of your sick parents ... You have consideration ... You're a real lady. (*Pause.*) We're both looking for someone ... something ... It's that goddam loneliness.

MEGAN. Books have cured my loneliness. I read everything I can find ... I'm transported to different lands .. different places ... One forgets when one reads.

HAROLD. The only book I ever read was *Moby Dick.*

MEGAN. Really?

HAROLD. And it was so damn long that I never finished it.

MEGAN. If you were in my class, I would have failed you. So you don't like to read, what are your hobbies? (*SHE sits.*)

HAROLD. I like sports ... going to baseball games ... football games ... I go fishing a lot ...

MEGAN. No foreign films, opera, or theater?

HAROLD. (*HE sits.*) Nah ... I suppose you go in for all that stuff.

MEGAN. Yes.

HAROLD. Don't you do something that's exciting?

MEGAN. I don't think you will find what I do exciting ... but I collect ticket stubs from movies ... I have jars and jars of these stubs ... Every time I go to a film, I keep the stub.

HAROLD. Are they worth anything?

MEGAN. Once I spoke to a collector about them. He just laughed. "ADMIT ONE" is printed on them so they don't have any value to anyone ... I like collecting them ... It just shows me that I've seen hundreds of movies ...

HAROLD. Well, you certainly are an unusual woman, Megan. (*Pause.*) I think we've gotten through everything.

MEGAN. (*Rises.*) Everything you want to know has been answered?

HAROLD. (*Rises.*) Yep ...

MEGAN. What happens now? Callbacks ... or do you send me a note saying, thanks, but no thanks? (*Pause.*) Can you tell me how I rated? On a scale from one to ten ... Do I get three, four, five?

HAROLD. I don't know about such things.

MEGAN. You're embarrassed, Mr. Conklin. And you feel embarrassed for me. It's obvious that we're not well-suited for each other. Our backgrounds are too different. No common ground ...

HAROLD. Wait! So you've been to hundreds of movies, seen places on those screens. I bet you I've *been* to those places on those screens. You read tons of books. I've *been* to those places in the books ...

MEGAN. I'd better go ... I enjoyed meeting you. It was an experience ... one that I will remember. What time do you have?

HAROLD. (*Checking watch.*) Four forty-five.

MEGAN. (*Looks at her watch.*) I'm still running slow. (*Pause.*) I'll be caught in the subway rush.

HAROLD. Well ... I don't know what to tell you. (*Pause.*) Smile. You've got a wonderful smile ... even when you're so grumpy ...

MEGAN. You're expecting somebody else ... That's why you're rushing me out.

HAROLD. No ... You've been rushing yourself out ever since you got here ... I don't know what's with you ... unless you got a husband already and you want to see if the grass can be greener ...

MEGAN. No ... it's not that.

HAROLD. Well, what is it, then?

MEGAN. It's nothing. (*Pause. SHE sits.*) Can I hear some music?

HAROLD. What?

MEGAN. The radio works?

HAROLD. Sure. (*HE turns on radio, and classical MUSIC plays.*) Is this okay?

MEGAN. It's fine.

HAROLD. So you're gonna sit and listen to this until the subway rush is over?

MEGAN. (*Rises.*) Do you want to dance, Mr. Conklin?

HAROLD. What?

MEGAN. Yes, dance. I told you I could. Now I'd like to—I don't want to leave here with you thinking I'm an eccentric woman who is boring. I'd like to give you a different impression of me ... I'd like to have some fun, Harold.

HAROLD. I'm game.

MEGAN. So let's dance. But we can't dance to classical music.

HAROLD. (*Switches stations, gets rock MUSIC.*) This mumbo-jumbo okay?

MEGAN. All right. Let's go!

(*THEY both start dancing, making up wild gestures as they go along and talk as THEY dance, sometimes shouting above the music.*)

HAROLD. You got real good balance for a dancer.

MEGAN. I'm improvising. I don't know what I'm doing ... really.

HAROLD. Hey, you're great! ... Megan, I smell that nice perfume on you ... the one your letter smelled of ... (*Pause.*) You have great legs ... not too many women have great legs.

MEGAN. I can't hear you!

HAROLD. Great legs! Great smell!

MEGAN. Thank you ...

HAROLD. Hey, are we gonna enter a contest?

MEGAN. I think we need practice ... Then maybe we'll win an award ... I like this dancing ... I know why people go to discos ... They just dance and it makes no sense, the music makes no sense ... so everything is not very clear ... It makes you forget ...

HAROLD. Is there something you want to forget, Megan?

MEGAN. (*Stops dancing. Sits on edge of bed.*) I'm getting tired. But that was so much fun ... I haven't had fun in ages ... But now I feel sort of dizzy.

HAROLD. (*Turns off music.*) Lie down on the bed.

MEGAN. (*Realizes where she's at and jumps up.*) Just a minute! Is this a final seduction scene?

HAROLD. What are you talking about now?

MEGAN. You try to seduce all the women who answered your ad!

HAROLD. Nah ...

MEGAN. I bet ... as soon as somebody feels tired, you point to the bed ... You think I'm some cheap date.

HAROLD. Now you're acting like a schoolteacher again. Just admit you had a good time and no back talk.

MEGAN. I did have a good time.

HAROLD. No crime to let your hair down ... or even lie down on the bed ... You can do whatever the hell you please ... Momma and Poppa are dead.

MEGAN. What time is it?

HAROLD. I told you just before. Why do you keep asking?

MEGAN. I have to go.

HAROLD. But you said you didn't want to be caught in the subway rush.

MEGAN. I know ... but I've been gone too long ... I won't be able to bring back a movie stub ... I didn't go to the movies.

HAROLD. What are you rambling about now?

MEGAN. I don't know what I'm doing here. I had no right coming here.

HAROLD. What?

MEGAN. You think I'm strange, don't you?

HAROLD. Well ... a little. But you didn't live the normal kind of life women lead. No, it's not your fault, mind you. I mean living with your parents that long ... You probably didn't bother with that many people, having to take care of them the way you did. How long have they been dead?

MEGAN. Not very long. (*Pause, then suddenly.*) Do you dream?

HAROLD. Sure do. When I dream, it's in color. And you know what my dreams are about—that everything is a nickel ... Five cents in bright, red letters!

MEGAN. (*Pause.*) What time do you have?

HAROLD. I don't know. My watch stopped.

MEGAN. It did not.

HAROLD. It did too. I've been looking at it too much. (*Pause.*) Megan, you know, you're too concerned with the time. Do you have somewhere to go?

MEGAN. No—I mean *yes.*

HAROLD. You're meeting another man?

MEGAN. No.

HAROLD. Then you're living with a man and you have to be home ... or maybe you're really married and this was just an adventure.

MEGAN. Yes, it was an adventure, something I never dared to do. But I don't live with a man and I'm not married.

HAROLD. So what's this about time?

MEGAN. I won't have the stub when I get back.

HAROLD. The stub?

MEGAN. The movie stub—that I told you I collect.

HAROLD. What do you need the stub for?

MEGAN. I need it ... desperately ... Maybe I can pick one up ... in the lobby ... Somewhere in a movie theater ... People do drop them ... Pick one up ... that'll be proof. Or if I can't find one, I'll simply buy one ... (*Pause. SHE starts to exit.*)

HAROLD. (*Blocking her.*) Just a minute, Megan. What's going on? There's somebody at your house, somebody you're afraid of ... not your husband or boyfriend ... (*Pause.*) Who is it?

MEGAN. Please, Harold ...

HAROLD. You need a movie stub. Who's going to punish you if you don't bring one home? (*Pause. HE thinks, suddenly realizes.*) Your parents?

MEGAN. Please!

HAROLD. They're living, aren't they?

MEGAN. No, I told you before they were dead.

HAROLD. I don't believe you ... They're alive ... And you're so afraid to go back without a movie stub. I'll be damned.

MEGAN. Harold, you're wrong.

HAROLD. No, I'm right. I figured it out, didn't I? Admit it, damn it!

MEGAN. No!

HAROLD. It's true, isn't it?

MEGAN. No! (*Goes towards door.*) I have to go!

HAROLD. (*Blocks doorway.*) Not until I hear the truth!

MEGAN. No!

HAROLD. Tell me!

MEGAN. I have nothing to tell you!

HAROLD. Your parents are living. They're waiting for you. They're going to punish you if you're not home. You're scared just like a little girl, Megan. You're shaking!

MEGAN. Stop tormenting me!

HAROLD. They're going to yell at you!

MEGAN. (*As if he were her parents.*) But I didn't do anything wrong! (*Sits. Pause.*) Please believe me! Don't be angry with me. I'm sorry. Forgive me, please!

HAROLD. You'll be forgiven, Megan. (*Pause. HE sits on chair.*) You can go now. Nobody's stopping you.

MEGAN. Thank you, Mr. Conklin.

HAROLD. You better go. You don't want them to worry too much.

MEGAN. Oh, no. They'll be angry if I'm gone too long. They worry and sicken ... You know, ever since I was little, they were sick ... They would always say, "We're not very well people ... You will always have to help us ... be good to us ... If you're not, God will take us away from you ..." And I would always take care of them because I was terrified that they would be taken away. I would be left all alone ... Here I am, now ... and I still have that same feeling ... They made me so afraid ... Now I'm frightened that I'm going to be all alone.

HAROLD. I don't believe this!

MEGAN. I hope I didn't take too much of your time. I was serious, believe me ... I had the best intentions by coming here ... But they're still alive.

HAROLD. Why'd you lie to me?

MEGAN. I only said they were dead because I didn't want you to know the truth. If you knew they were alive you would want to know why I came here. I had no reason to come here if my parents are still living and I'm taking care of them ... Being a saint is a miraculous thing ... but it can also be a burden ... It's wearing ... I've done it out of duty ... I sacrificed my life for them. (*Pause.*) I look at them sleeping at night, their bodies look so stiff ... And I think, should I cover them, put blankets over their faces? But I'm a saint and saints aren't killers ... So I just go out of their room and in the morning we all smile at each other ... They tell me how good I am ... how they couldn't go on without me. (*Pause*.) Once I tried to leave ... had everything packed ... had an apartment picked out ... They talked me out of it ... They said I shouldn't go ... too expensive ... They would get very sick if I left ... I might get sick too ... So I unpacked slowly and I stayed ... That was twenty years ago ... I was thirty-nine.

HAROLD. (*Softly stunned*.) Then you're fifty-nine ... You told me you were forty-nine.

MEGAN. My memory has failed me ... If there is one thing that has failed me, it's memory.

HAROLD. All these lies, Megan ... about your age, about your parents ...

MEGAN. I just wanted to be accepted. You are the first man I've had an appointment with in five years.

HAROLD. It's all right, Megan. (*Pause*.) I know wh..t you're saying. You've been living in the The Stone Age.

MEGAN. That's why I might seem a bit odd to you. I've been too isolated ... for a very long time ... I was going, wasn't I? I was supposed to be leaving before ... I shouldn't be here now ...

HAROLD. Take it easy ...

MEGAN. All those movie stubs ... Over two thousand "ADMIT ONE's."

(*Silence*.)

HAROLD. I just don't know what to say.

MEGAN. The next woman that you interview ... you will tell her all about me. You'll both laugh or feel sorry.

HAROLD. Trust me, I won't say a word. Do you think anyone would believe me?

MEGAN. You see, you *do* think I'm strange.

HAROLD. (*Rises.*) Look, you might not believe it ... But I know how you feel ... Oh, you have the degrees and the big words ... but the feelings are the same ... I like you ... And I don't think you're crazy or weird.

MEGAN. What does that mean?

HAROLD. It means that it's not too late, Megan.

MEGAN. For what?

HAROLD. To leave them.

MEGAN. (*Rises.*) Oh, no! It would be a sacrilege.

HAROLD. You're just running scared. Maybe that's why you took care of them so long ... Maybe you just didn't want to strike out on your own.

MEGAN. No, they make me feel obligated to them ... I told you, ever since I was a child ...

HAROLD. Do they chain you down?

MEGAN. Imaginary emotional chains are stronger than physical ones.

HAROLD. Bull! Face life, Megan.

MEGAN. You think you're an analyst.

HAROLD. Nah, I don't believe in that crap. I have common sense and that's what tells me things.

MEGAN. I'm a recluse ... just going out occasionally for a breath of fresh air.

HAROLD. (*Pause.*) My house is near the ocean ... the air is better there than in Flushing.

MEGAN. We have nothing in common ... Different interests, different backgrounds.

HAROLD. That's for sure ... You've only been to parts of New Jersey ... Whoever heard of something like that? I'll tell you all about my travels ... and you can tell me about the movies and books ... (*Pause.*) I'll understand ... believe me.

MEGAN. There's something very kind about you ... Hal.

HAROLD. I know. (*Realizes.*) You called me Hal.

MEGAN. So I did.

HAROLD. Megan, I'd like to see you again.

MEGAN. (*Sits.*) You would?

HAROLD. Sure, we'll go out on a date.

MEGAN. (*Rises.*) I don't know ...

HAROLD. Don't worry, I'll get you plenty of movie stubs.

MEGAN. Well ...

HAROLD. I'd like to get to know you better. I guess it's the gentleman in me.

MEGAN. I'm still not sure.

HAROLD. How about it? (*Pause.*) I'll tell you what. I'll make you a deal. I'll even finish *Moby Dick* for you. (*HE smiles at her. SHE smiles back. LIGHTS slowly fade to black.*)

COSTUME PLOT

HAROLD CONKLIN: A spiffy looking suit
                          A pocket handkerchief
                          Colorful but
                              conservative tie
                          Wristwatch
                          Dark socks
                          Dress shoes

MEGAN MATTHEWS: Tasteful dress, very
                              feminine, not too
                              dressy
                          Clutch purse
                          Wristwatch
                          Nylons
                          Low heels

PROPERTY PLOT

Set Pieces: Bed
                   Nightstand with lamp
                   Bureau (or table)
                   Two chairs

Props: (Pre-set)   <u>On Bureau:</u>
                   A paper bag containing two
                       full wine bottles
                   Two small plastic glasses
                   Stack of letters

                   <u>On Nightstand:</u>
                   Radio (a working one)

HAROLD: Inside jacket pocket:
                       Letter on pink stationery
                   In hip pocket, wallet
                       containing: two photos

Optional: <u>On Walls:</u>
                   A picture hanging
                       crookedly
                   Window
                   Mirror over bureau
                   (If there are no walls, the
                   above can be imaginary)

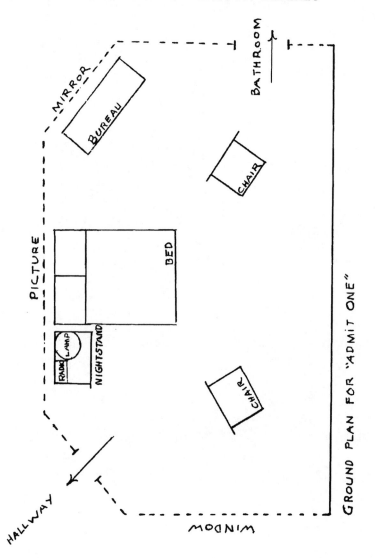

THE CAT CONNECTION

The Cat Connection was presented in Love Creek Productions' One-Act Festival at The Cubiculo in New York City in 1988, directed by Cathy Caster, with the following cast:

MAY REYNOLDS .... Toni Genfan Brown
LEONA WOODS.................................... Diane Hoblit

The play has also been presented by The Cultural Environ's Drama Workshop for Older Adults, N.Y.C., and then toured senior citizen centers in Queens, New York.

CHARACTERS

MAY REYNOLDS   late sixties, looks fed-up
                             and tired, a bit on the
                             untidy side.

LEONA WOODS   late sixties, is high-strung,
                             nervous, but keeps herself
                             together very well.

TIME
The present. Spring. Very early evening.

PLACE
Any park bench, in any city.

THE CAT CONNECTION

SCENE: A park bench.

AT RISE: MAY enters, wearing an old dress. SHE carries a pocketbook and a small paper bag.

MAY. (*Sits down wearily, then from the paper bag, SHE takes an opened can of cat food, and sets it on the ground, then crumples paper bag and throws it under the bench.*) Another day has gone by ... soon another night ... then tomorrow another day ... Are you around, Whiskey? If you are, I got food for you. If you're not, well, that's life ... Here ... (*Calling.*) Pssss ... Pssss ...

(*LEONA enters, dressed very neatly, carrying a purse and shopping bag.*)

LEONA. Who are you and what are you doing here?
MAY. I can ask you the same questions.
LEONA. I heard you calling, "Pssss ... Pssss ..."
MAY. I was ... Is that a crime?
LEONA. No.
MAY. (*Calling again.*) Pssss ... Pssss ...

LEONA. (*Looking at cat food.*) So you're feeding a cat?

MAY. You gonna arrest me?

LEONA. I would like to know what kind of cat you're feeding.

MAY. Are you with the police or something?

LEONA. No. I would just like to know if it's—(*SHE sets shopping bag carefully on the ground and takes from it a small dish which is covered with a napkin.*)

MAY. (*Interrupting.*) What do you have under that napkin?

LEONA. (*Uncovering it proudly.*) Tuna fish. Real tuna fish.

MAY. The kind that humans eat?

LEONA. (*Sets dish on ground.*) That's right.

MAY. And you're gonna give it to a cat?

LEONA. Yes.

MAY. That cat gets cat food tuna fish from me.

LEONA. (*Sits close to May on bench and folds napkin, places it back in the shopping bag.*) Please tell me about the cat you're feeding.

MAY. (*Inching away.*) Why?

LEONA. I want to know if it's the same one. Is she a gray and white striped one with a patch of black on her nose?

MAY. These strays look all the same to me

LEONA. Does she have very long whiskers?

MAY. Lady, I never examined her.

LEONA. Does she sometimes take the food with her paw?

MAY. (*Softening.*) Yes.

LEONA. Then we're feeding the same one. Have you seen her?

MAY. Not yet.

LEONA. How long have you been sitting here?

MAY. Not even five minutes when you came along.

LEONA. I've never seen you around here before.

MAY. I'm usually around earlier.

LEONA. How long have you been feeding her?

MAY. I don't know. A couple of weeks.

LEONA. It's been nearly two months for me.

MAY. That long? (*Calling.*) Pssss. Whiskey.

LEONA. Whiskey?

MAY. That's her name.

LEONA. Her name is Cleopatra.

MAY. Maybe that's what you call her. To me, she's Whiskey.

LEONA. That's not a very dignified name for a cat.

MAY. Oh, pardon me. I forgot this is a royal cat that eats regular tuna fish.

LEONA. I give her food that I eat ... Shrimp ... chicken ... white meat only.

MAY. What do you know? A high-class cat.

LEONA. Cleopatra deserves the best.

MAY. If you think she's so special, why don't you just take her home?

LEONA. I can't just yet. She's pregnant.

MAY. Pregnant? I thought she was just a fat cat.

LEONA. I took her to the vet to make sure. He said within the next week, which means any day now—she'll have a litter—between six and twelve kittens.

MAY. No kidding?

LEONA. I can't bring her home now because I already have four cats.

MAY. Four?

LEONA. Yes. Charlemagne, Catherine the Great, Queen of Sheba and James the Tenth.

MAY. What a group!

LEONA. They're darling. Did you know that our sixteenth President, Mr. Abraham Lincoln, had four cats in the White House? However, I don't know what their names were.

MAY. Are you thinking of running for President?

LEONA. No. I'm just telling you a little-known fact about cats. They're appreciated by some of the most powerful people throughout history.

MAY. Well, you learn something new every day ... (*Pause.*) I don't know why you just don't bring that pregnant cat home. Think of all your power with twelve more cats.

LEONA. My cats would resent Cleopatra. They have their own territory. Besides, they all have very sharp claws ... It's not a good idea now. But I have her future all mapped out.

MAY. You do?

LEONA. After Cleopatra has her kittens, I have arranged for a couple who takes care of strays to house all of them. After a month, I will take Cleopatra home with me.

MAY. You got the whole thing planned out?

LEONA. Yes.

MAY. I couldn't stand to have one cat in my house. I don't like them creeping around. I get the chills.

LEONA. It doesn't sound like you like cats very much. Why are you feeding this one?

MAY. Oh, just to pass some time. Cats are all right as long as they're not in my house.

LEONA. (*Calling.*) Here ... Cleopatra ... please come here.

MAY. Maybe she's mad at you.

LEONA. For what? She knows when I come around. She's used to this place, at this time. She knows my scent. Maybe she's not coming around because you're here.

MAY. Nah ...

LEONA. I've been feeding her regularly at this time.

MAY. You act like she can tell time or something. Cats are real dumb and not too loyal. I heard about this eighty-year-old woman who had a cat for years. One day she just forgot to feed it and the cat came after her at night, clawed her to death in her sleep.

LEONA. I don't believe it.

MAY. It's the truth. So watch out for your group at home and this one too.

LEONA. (*Pause.*) She must be confused seeing two people here at once.

MAY. You see Whiskey?

LEONA. Cleopatra may see us.

MAY. If she was around, she'd be out here. She'd smell the food. Maybe she had her kittens somewhere and you'll never find out where.

LEONA. Would you mind leaving?

MAY. This is a public place and a free country.

LEONA. I know.

MAY. No, you don't, because you're telling me to leave.

LEONA. Only for Cleopatra's good. What I'm saying is that I have her food. Stop by later.

MAY. No. I'm gonna sit right here.

LEONA. Why do you insist on being so stubborn?

MAY. I was here first.

LEONA. Yes, you were.

MAY. So if anybody should leave, it should be you.

LEONA. I will not.

MAY. Why don't you stop making a big deal out of this? Either that cat will come around or it won't.

LEONA. What do you mean by that?

MAY. It has nothing to do with me being here.

LEONA. I'm not so sure. There's a shyness about her, a coyness. She seems to be saying, "I don't want to be around more than one person in my condition."

MAY. She told you that?

LEONA. Yes.

MAY. Lady, if you tell anybody that, they'll think you're crazy.

LEONA. She didn't actually speak to me.

MAY. That's good to know.

LEONA. Her eyes told me. I never saw anything like it before. The way she looks at me. I could read her mind. More than any other cat I know. Cleopatra knows that I realize it. Her beautiful yellow eyes know I understand everything.

MAY. I wouldn't go around telling that to people.

LEONA. When she sits in my lap, I can feel a certain connection. I feel so calm. My blood pressure goes down. It has wonderful healing powers.

MAY. It's a stray, that's all. It looks like a million other cats. Nothing special, no powers. A cat is a cat, nothing more. Those stripes, those eyes, those whiskers ... I can't tell the difference.

LEONA. How can you say something like that? You've been feeding her a few weeks.

MAY. So?

LEONA. After all that time, you'd think you'd know the difference.

MAY. What's the big deal?

LEONA. Don't you find Cleopatra very appreciative when you feed her?

MAY. That's for sure. It licks my leg and purrs in my face.

LEONA. Of course, she's very grateful to you and me. Animals are more appreciative than people. I learned that a long time ago. They will never disappoint you but people will. One time when I was a young woman, this teenager came over to me and asked me to help her make a phone call from a phone booth, so I did. The next thing I knew was my pocketbook was gone and so was she. From that time on, I never trusted people, put all my faith in cats.

MAY. Maybe you're right but I can't get excited over the cat the way you do.

LEONA. (*Impatient.*) Where is she? Why isn't she here by now?

MAY. Maybe she met with foul play.

LEONA. Foul play?

MAY. She could have run into a German shepherd.

LEONA. Oh no!

MAY. Or it could have been hit by a car.

LEONA. I'd never forgive myself. Why don't you stop this?

MAY. Take it easy, it's only a cat.

LEONA. She won't disappoint me. I'll just apply some more perfume. My scent will be stronger. (*Takes small perfume bottle out of purse and dabs some on.*)

MAY. What's that stuff?

LEONA. It's called *Breathless Power*.

MAY. You're not kidding!

LEONA. Cleopatra knows my scent and she'll be around.

MAY. I'm sure that will bring her out from anywhere.

(*THEY wait.*)

LEONA. I also have her flea powder. (*Puts perfume back in purse, and then takes a can of flea powder from her shopping bag.*)

MAY. (*Aghast.*) Flea powder? She's got fleas? I'm not gonna touch her anymore.

LEONA. Don't be silly. Every few days I rub it all over her. (*Indicates powder.*) Then she sits right in my lap. She likes to be stroked around the neck.

MAY. The pleasure is all yours.

LEONA. (*Putting powder back in shopping bag.*) She's not picking up on my perfume. I'm going to look for her. Do me a favor? Wait right here. (*Rises.*)

MAY. Now you don't want me to leave?

LEONA. Maybe she'll come out when I'm gone. If you leave, I'll never know. Please do me this favor.

MAY. (*Reluctant.*) All right, I'll stay.

LEONA. (*Taking out "cat treats" from shopping bag.*) Thanks. Now if she comes out just give her one of these cat treats ... (*Hands them to May.*) to keep her attention. I'll be right back. (*SHE exits.*)

MAY. (*Looks at cat treats, rises and calls.*) Whiskey ... here ... Whiskey ... some goodies for you. But don't come too close. (*Looks in shopping bag, takes out rubber ball.*) Do you want to play, huh? Or are you having your kittens somewhere? All twelve ... You're missing out on some very good tuna fish. All right, be that way. (*Puts ball and "cat treats" back in shopping bag.*) Whiskey, you know, in spite of the fact that you're a bad cat, you help me forget. (*Sits, takes out a pint whiskey bottle from her pocketbook, takes several swigs, then puts it away.*) Ahh ... that really hits the spot. (*Now SHE begins to act silly.*) Oh, you bad, bad cat ... Come out, wherever you are ... Heh ... Heh ... Red light, green light ... boo ... (*Rises, moving around.*) Oh, cat ... Please come out ... We're going crazy waiting for you ... Yoo-hoo ... Where are you hiding? If you come out, you will get a whole bag full of goodies ... I'll count to ten ... 10, 9, 8, 7, 6, 5, 4, 3, 2 ... Cat, the water-rat ... the fat cat ... fat cat, bad cat, spat cat ... And now 1. Did you hear that, Whiskey, now 1? I've counted to ten, come out now ... or else you won't get all your goodies ... Drat on you, you flea-bag cat ... (*Dances around.*)

LEONA. (*Re-enters.*) I didn't have any luck ... so many bushes ... I don't know where to begin. (*Now staring at her.*) Just what are you doing?

MAY. What does it look like I'm doing? I'm doing a dance so that Whiskey will come out ... Whew ...

(*SHE feels dizzy. LEONA helps her to sit down and sits down herself.*)

LEONA. Are you okay?

MAY. Just a little dizzy. But I feel great!

LEONA. (*Taken aback*.) You smell of whiskey.

MAY. Nah.

LEONA. You do.

MAY. So I took a little nip, that's all.

LEONA. It smells like more than a nip. Now I understand why you named her Whiskey.

MAY. Whiskey the cat makes me feel a little better. And whiskey the drink does too.

LEONA. You shouldn't drink.

MAY. I'm a big girl. I'm over twenty-one.

LEONA. That's beside the point. It'll get you sick.

MAY. One sip here and there—

LEONA. Leads to more.

MAY. Why don't you just mind your own business?

LEONA. I'm trying to be of some help.

MAY. Go help your cat.

LEONA. I couldn't find her. I'm so upset.

MAY. You're gonna give yourself a stroke over an alley cat. Who told her to get pregnant?

LEONA. She couldn't help it.

MAY. I have no pity for her. Hundreds of cats roaming around, getting pregnant, every day and night.

LEONA. I'm beginning to think she has given birth somewhere. I'll never know where. So many bushes in the park.

MAY. What are you gonna do?

LEONA. What can I do? I just feel very guilty. I should have taken her in.

MAY. How can anybody get so upset over an animal? I could see if it's a person. (*Pause. SHE curls up on bench.*)

LEONA. Don't fall asleep here.

MAY. I'm tired. That liquor really works— makes me want to just fade out for the night.

LEONA. Maybe you should just go home.

MAY. I don't want to go home right now. I'll just watch the TV. And that makes me more lonesome. It's not the same anymore. Nothing is the same anymore.

LEONA. What do you mean?

MAY. (*Sits up.*) Since he left.

LEONA. Who?

MAY. Wally, he was my husband. Three weeks ago, he walked out on me ... Ever since then, I'm not feeling so good. I went walking a lot ... And I sat in this park ... I heard this cat meowing ... I felt sorry so I brought her food. She licked me. I felt better. And I showed up the next day and the very next day after that ... Somebody was waiting for me ... Now the dirty cat is gone. I don't think that cat will come back.

LEONA. Don't say that.

MAY. Face it. Just like I know Wally's never coming back. (*Pause.*) He ran away. Three weeks ago, I come home and there's this note pasted to the refrigerator. It says, "May, I can't take this marriage anymore." Now, mind you, the man is seventy-three years old. Well, I couldn't believe it. We're married fifty years. I checked his clothes. They were gone. His suitcase was gone. Next thing I looked at was our bankbook but nothing was taken out. I called the police. I thought he was kidnapped or something. No trace of him. Then a week later, I get this letter from Hawaii. It was from him. He wrote and told me the whole story. He was planning to leave me from the day he married me.

LEONA. What?

MAY. Yeah, imagine him planning it all along. He was getting ready for his late-life crisis for years.

LEONA. I'm sorry this happened to you.

MAY. You know what the sly devil did? He had his own back account. For fifty years since we were married, he would go to the bank and deposit one dollar, just one lonesome dollar a day. And it added up over the years. So now he's in Hawaii. I should have known he was up to something. When he'd see pictures of Hawaii in the magazines, he would say, "May, that's paradise. I want to live in paradise before I pass on." I bet he's walking around with those funny-looking things you wear around your neck and those flashy-colored shirts.

LEONA. Oh my! I never heard anything quite like this.

MAY. I bet one of those gossip newspapers would grab it.

LEONA. It has to be more bizarre.

MAY. (*As if reading from headline*.) "Seventy-three-year-old man runs away from wife but ends up trapped in volcano in Hawaii."

LEONA. (*Also as if reading*.) "Buried alive in the fiery lava ... which sizzles into the sea!"

MAY. Yeah. Maybe that will happen to him. I pray it happens. All I know is that I don't sleep the way I used to. The doctor prescribed sleeping pills but I don't want nothing like that. So he says, "Take a glass of warm milk, that'll do the trick," But that's what I used to do when I was a girl. So now I take whiskey ... works wonders ... puts me right to sleep.

LEONA. It's not the answer.

MAY. Right now it is ... You know, I never touched the stuff my whole life ... till now ... It takes my mind off things ... If it works for me, why not? As mad as I am at him, I'm not used to him not being around. After fifty years, I can't get used to being alone.

LEONA. Just busy yourself, that's all. The main point of life is to be busy.

MAY. With what?

LEONA. Even the smallest things. Did you ever watch the sky getting dark, then light? Or how it is different shades of white, gray, and blue?

MAY. Who cares?

LEONA. It's interesting to see.

MAY. Is that how you have your fun?

LEONA. It's a way of passing time and it's pleasant. If we only took the very ordinary things of life and paid more attention to them, we'd all be a lot happier. Like the way flowers have different colors and shapes. The way leaves turn according to the seasons ... the way that cars go by at different speeds.

MAY. Who ever thinks of those things?

LEONA. That's my point.

MAY. (*Pause.*) You know, if he ever came back, I don't think I'd take him back. I've got my pride. The good thing was he left me money. He wasn't a total louse.

LEONA. He wasn't.

MAY. At times like these, it would be nice to get some kind words from children—but we never had any.

LEONA. If Cleopatra gives birth, think of yourself as her stepmother.

MAY. I think we won't see that cat anymore.

LEONA. I won't give up hope.

MAY. Why don't you go home? Your cats will be worried.

LEONA. My cats are fine.

MAY. (*Pause.*) You're not married?

LEONA. No ... But my cat family keeps me very busy. And I'm still working three days as a waitress.

MAY. At your age?

LEONA. Yes. I suppose I'll work till I drop the plates. But I still have my strength. I don't like to sit around all day. But people are getting cheaper all the time. On a twenty-four dollar check, I get one dollar. Imagine! From three people! In the morning, I sometimes get a nickel on a breakfast check.

MAY. Maybe you should work in a different place.

LEONA. In a lot of places, they only like the young ones. So I have to be thankful that I have a job.

MAY. All your life you worked as a waitress?

LEONA. Yes.

MAY. You must work very hard.

LEONA. I do.

MAY. But you see people all day and talk to them. I never see anyone. Wally and me never had any friends. We were always together. So we never needed nobody else. Now I'm all alone. You must have have a lot of friends.

LEONA. Just because I serve people all day, doesn't mean that I have a lot of friends. I'm sick of people by the time I come home.

MAY. You have no friends either?

LEONA. Who needs anyone? After a day's work, I come home and have my four cats waiting at the door, all of them there to greet me ... purring and licking me all over. It makes my evening.

MAY. You never wanted to get married?

LEONA. I did. I was engaged when I was twenty.

MAY. What happened?

LEONA. (*Pause.*) The young man got strep throat. Years ago, there was no such thing as antibiotics. The infection went to his eyes. He went blind and had to be put away in a home. I visited him all the time. I still loved him and wanted to marry him. But he was too full of self-pity. One day he ended it all. I never forgot him. So I thought it was better off to remain alone, devote time to animals.

MAY. That's got to be one of the saddest stories I ever heard. It's even sadder than mine. At least, I had fifty good years with Wally. (*Pause.*) So you never met anybody else?

LEONA. It took me many years to get over John. I never wanted to meet anybody else. Who wanted to suffer again?

MAY. You would have really married that blind man?

LEONA. Yes, but he didn't want me to. He didn't want to spoil my life.

MAY. (*Takes out whiskey.*) I think I need another shot. How about you?

LEONA. No, thank you. I wish you wouldn't drink anymore. That's how I started, a sip here, a sip there. To drown out the pain ... and the drinking got worse. It all started from a nip.

MAY. You mean you were a drinker?

LEONA. That was the only way I could block out my pain ... after I lost John.

MAY. (*Looking at bottle.*) If I have any more, I might pass out. (*Puts it away.*)

LEONA. On your way home, why don't you just decide to throw it away?

MAY. Maybe I will.

LEONA. (*Pause*.) You know what? I think you're right, that we've seen the last of Cleopatra.

MAY. I've been telling you that all along.

LEONA. After all that I did for her ... Fed her for two whole months, took her to the vet, made future arrangements. She just didn't care.

MAY. She doesn't know any better.

LEONA. Could it be that cats are getting to be like people, unappreciative?

MAY. Maybe she's just giving birth somewhere. And couldn't make it today.

LEONA. I'd feel better if that were true.

MAY. She'll be all right.

LEONA. I know. Cats know how to take care of themselves. They're very resourceful. They're survivors. At least it's spring, not winter. She and her kittens will be nice and warm. Her kittens will grow up and become cats and they'll all roam around somewhere and Cleopatra will be around, too.

MAY. I bet she'll be naughty again. And her kittens will, too. The cat population will never stop growing.

LEONA. (*Laughing*.) You're right. (*Pause*.) I'd better be going home. My cat family is waiting for me ... (*Looks at her tuna fish on ground*.) My Charlemagne will eat this. (*Takes out napkin, covers dish again and replaces it in shopping bag*.)

MAY. (*Picking up her can from ground*.) You could take my food for one of your other cats. But it's just regular cat food tuna.

LEONA. That's all right. Even though The Queen of Sheba is royalty, she insists on just plain cat food. (*Takes can from May.*) But maybe we should leave this—just in case. (*SHE sets May's can back on ground.*) You know, here we are talking all this time. I don't even know your name.

MAY. May Reynolds.

LEONA. Pleased to meet you, May. (*SHE stands up with shopping bag and extends her hand.*) I'm Leona Woods.

(*MAY takes her hand as SHE rises. THEY smile and after a moment exit together.*)

BLACKOUT

COSTUME PLOT

MAY REYNOLDS	An old dress Socks Casual shoes or sneakers
LEONA WOODS	White blouse Dark skirt Stockings Casual shoes

PROPERTY PLOT

Set Piece: A park bench (or
                                    the bench could be
                                    suggested by a row
                                    of straight chairs).

PERSONAL PROPS:

MAY REYNOLDS: Small paper bag
                                    containing: opened
                                    can of cat food;
                                    Pocketbook
                                    containing: pint
                                    whiskey bottle

LEONA WOODS: An attractive
                                    shopping bag
                                    containing: small
                                    dish suggesting
                                    "tuna fish,"
                                    covered with
                                    napkin; Can of flea
                                    powder; Rubber
                                    ball; "Cat treats".
                                    Purse containing:
                                    small perfume
                                    bottle

PARK BENCH

GROUND PLAN FOR "THE CAT CONNECTION"

OTHER TITLES AVAILABLE FROM SAMUEL FRENCH

CAPTIVE
Jan Buttram

Comedy / 2m, 1f / Interior

A hilarious take on a father/daughter relationship, this off beat comedy combines foreign intrigue with down home philosophy. Sally Pound flees a bad marriage in New York and arrives at her parent's home in Texas hoping to borrow money from her brother to pay a debt to gangsters incurred by her husband. Her elderly parents are supposed to be vacationing in Israel, but she is greeted with a shotgun aimed by her irascible father who has been left home because of a minor car accident and is not at all happy to see her. When a news report indicates that Sally's mother may have been taken captive in the Middle East, Sally's hard-nosed brother insists that she keep father home until they receive definite word, and only then will he loan Sally the money. Sally fails to keep father in the dark, and he plans a rescue while she finds she is increasingly unable to skirt the painful truths of her life. The ornery father and his loveable but slightly-dysfunctional daughter come to a meeting of hearts and minds and solve both their problems.

OTHER TITLES AVAILABLE FROM SAMUEL FRENCH

TAKE HER, SHE'S MINE
Phoebe and Henry Ephron

Comedy / 11m, 6f / Various Sets

Art Carney and Phyllis Thaxter played the Broadway roles of parents of two typical American girls enroute to college. The story is based on the wild and wooly experiences the authors had with their daughters, Nora Ephron and Delia Ephron, themselves now well known writers. The phases of a girl's life are cause for enjoyment except to fearful fathers. Through the first two years, the authors tell us, college girls are frightfully sophisticated about all departments of human life. Then they pass into the "liberal" period of causes and humanitarianism, and some into the intellectual lethargy of beatniksville. Finally, they start to think seriously of their lives as grown ups. It's an experience in growing up, as much for the parents as for the girls.

"A warming comedy. A delightful play about parents vs kids. It's loaded with laughs. It's going to be a smash hit."
– *New York Mirror*